DATE DUE

AUG 1 02			
SEP 3 02			
GAYLORD			PRINTED IN U.S.A.

BUILT FOR SPEED

DRAG RACER

Matthew Pitt

HIGH
interest
books

Children's Press
A Division of Grolier Publishing

Book Design: Christopher Logan
Contributing Editor: Jeri Cipriano

Photo Credits: pp. 5, 16, 20, 21, 23, 26, 33, 38, 40, 41 ® Jon Asher; pp. 6, 8, 10, 13, 14 ® www.nitroparts.com; pp. 19, 30 ® AP Photo Archive/BenMargot; p. 29 ® AP Photo Archive/Auto Imagery, Inc.; pp. 24, 36 ® Allsport/Jamie Squire; p. 34 ® Allsport/Mike Powell

Visit Children's Press on the Internet at:
http://publishing.grolier.com

Library of Congress Cataloging-in-Publication Data

Pitt, Matthew.
    Drag racer / by Matthew Pitt.
      p. cm. — (Built for speed)
    Includes bibliographical references and index.
    ISBN 0-516-23159-6 (lib. bdg.) — ISBN 0-516-23262-2 (pbk.)
    1. Drag racing—Juvenile literature. [1. Drag racer.] I. Title. II.
Built for speed

GV1029.3 .P58 2000
796.72'0973—dc21

                                                00-063900

CONTENTS

INTRODUCTION

The stadium is packed. Fifty thousand eyes focus on a single strip of track. No one in the audience dares to look away. Everyone is motionless, waiting for the race to begin. Wheels screech and spin. The sharp smell of burning rubber fills the air.

On the track, the drivers of the Top Fuel dragsters are ready. They focus on the band of colored lights in front of them. The instant the lights switch from amber to green, they peel out.

Drag racing tests the nerves. It is motor sports' version of a sprint run—sheer speed. If a driver blinks or hesitates, he or she could lose the race. Drag races are over in just seconds.

A Top Fuel dragster zooms down the track.

When dragsters burn across the track at full speed, they look like bright blurs of color. This book will explain how drag racing got its start. You'll see how dragster cars work. Finally, you'll learn how you can watch and participate in this thrilling sport.

At the STARTING Line

Drag racing began in the western United States. In the 1930s, restless Californians began challenging each other to races. One driver would say he had the fastest car in the state. A second driver would overhear. Before you knew it, a race was on.

Drag racing competitions were easier to participate in than some other forms of racing. People didn't have to spend money on new cars. They just improved the ones they already owned.

Drivers fixed up their engines and transmissions so their cars would accelerate, or pick up speed faster. They didn't need a fancy racetrack, either. They just used the longest street in town. Of course, back in the 1930s, California towns didn't have many streets. So drivers competed on flat stretches of dirt.

Here is a drag race from 1954. It was sponsored by the National Hot Rod Association.

After World War II (1939–1945), drag races took place on empty military airfields or in giant parking lots. Drag racing competitions didn't require a lot of space, time, or money. The drivers lived in the slower and more open parts of the country. But they were breaking all the speed records.

Newspapers called these first drag racers hot-rodders. Hot-rodders raced to win, but they were happy when a friend sped to victory and into the record books.

The idea of speed didn't just appeal to hot-rodders. It also excited people who wanted to see a good race. Many people would come to drag races. Their cheering was nearly as loud as the rumble from the engines.

GOOD VISION

One of drag racing's biggest fans was Wally Parks. Parks was a racer who lived in California. When he wasn't racing, he

These hot-rodders, in 1959, are proud of the car that they built.

During a race in Irwindale, California, this dragster's engine caught fire. Thankfully, the driver was okay.

watched others race. Parks didn't approve of everything that he saw. He began to worry about problems that were sneaking into his beloved sport.

Cars were becoming less safe. Explosions and spinouts were common. Some drivers, called shot-rodders, turned to thievery. They broke into garages and stole parts for their hot rods. So in 1951, Wally Parks formed a group known as the National Hot Rod Association (NHRA). Thanks to the NHRA, drag racing became safer. Racers were required to wear helmets. Cars were equipped with roll bars. These kept drivers from getting hurt if the cars flipped.

Parks used NHRA membership money to award prizes and begin a championship called the Nationals. This event was held at a new spot each year so that people in different parts of the country would be exposed to the sport. As the safety of dragsters improved, so did cars' performances. In the early 1950s, hot rods began to exceed 100 mph (161 km/h). Because of Wally Parks's vision, drag racing became a national hit.

"BIG DADDY"

As drag racing became more popular, racing fans began to regard the drivers as celebrities. Drivers were given wild nicknames, such as Freight Train and Time Machine. One driver began calling himself The Snake. Another driver got sick of reading articles about The Snake all the time. So he nicknamed himself The Mongoose—a snake's natural enemy!

The biggest drag racing hero of the 1950s was Don "Big Daddy" Garlits. He won races and broke speed records every year. But Garlits was more than just a thrilling driver.

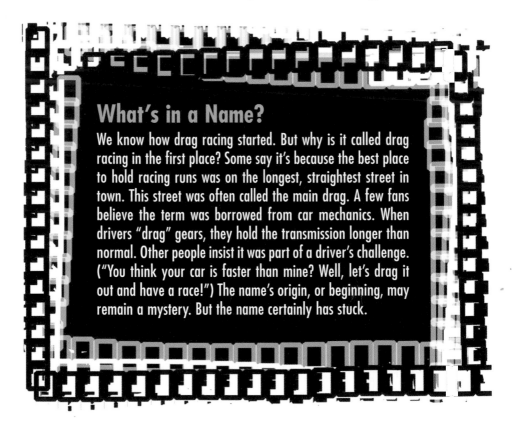

What's in a Name?

We know how drag racing started. But why is it called drag racing in the first place? Some say it's because the best place to hold racing runs was on the longest, straightest street in town. This street was often called the main drag. A few fans believe the term was borrowed from car mechanics. When drivers "drag" gears, they hold the transmission longer than normal. Other people insist it was part of a driver's challenge. ("You think your car is faster than mine? Well, let's drag it out and have a race!") The name's origin, or beginning, may remain a mystery. But the name certainly has stuck.

One of the superstars of drag racing was Don "Big Daddy" Garlits. Here he is racing his Wynn's Jammer dragster.

He was an innovator. He improved the design and mechanics of dragsters. When Garlits first started drag racing, engines were placed in the front of the cars. During one race, Garlits's car engine caught fire. His foot was badly burned. But Garlits refused to give up. He designed a new dragster, placing the engine in the back. This design made dragsters safer. Rear-engine hot rods are standard today.

Other innovations helped make this era exciting. The chassis, or frame, of hot rods was designed to be lighter. Also, wider tires were created that had gummy surfaces. These tires produced greater grip, or traction, on the drag strip.

Innovators in the 1950s changed the sport of drag racing forever. Drivers and mechanics always were tinkering with their cars. They would adjust a cylinder head, or the carburetor, just a hair. They would stay up all night to increase the cars' speed just a little bit more. They began to try different fuels in their hot rods. They found that, although regular gasoline worked well, other mixtures worked better.

All these small differences began to separate one hot rod from the next until it wasn't fair for certain cars to race. The NHRA decided to divide hot rods into groups. This is called classification. Today, there are more than two hundred classes of dragsters. The

Mechanics get a dragster ready for a race in 1955.

three most popular are the Top Fuel, Funny Car, and Pro Stock categories. The fastest and most familiar of the three is the Top Fuel.

NEEDLE ON THE GROOVE

The shape of Top Fuel dragsters should be familiar. They are long and low to the ground. They become pointed toward the nose, like a needle. Top Fuel cars are shaped this way for a reason. This special shape helps them cut through the strong winds that hit them during a race. It improves their aerodynamics. Aerodynamics is a measure of how air affects an object's movement. If a hot rod isn't aero-dynamic, wind can't flow smoothly over it, and the dragster's speed suffers.

You also can see a fixed wing at the rear of all Top Fuel cars. This wing is known as an airfoil. Its job is to press the high winds into the ground. This creates a type of energy called downforce. Downforce keeps Top Fuel cars firmly on the

Top Fuel dragsters have wings to help keep them on the track.

track. It also helps hot-rod drivers stay in control.

Although there are two hundred classes of dragsters, all drag races are run in the same way. They take place on long straightaways. Straightaways are strips of track without curves. The strips are one quarter of a mile long (1,320 feet). They're different from tracks like the ones at the Indianapolis 500, which are oval and have many turns. Drag runs begin at one end of the strip. When the light signals green, dragsters take off from a standing start. This means they begin the race at 0 miles per hour. But it takes only 1 second for Top Fuel cars to go from 0 to 100 mph (161 km/h). Races last less than 5 seconds. By the time the race is over, hot rods will have accelerated to speeds of more than 300 mph (483 km/h)!

THE WHEEL DEAL

There is another reason why Top Fuel dragsters are built with that narrow, needlelike

It only takes 1 second for a Top Fuel dragster to go from 0 to 100 mph (161 km/h).

shape. An area of sticky rubber covers the center of drag strips. This is the track's groove. Hot-rodders want their Top Fuel cars to stay on this groove. It is where the tires have the best traction. But the groove is only 8 feet (2.4 m) wide. By making the hot rod less than 5 feet (1.5 m) wide, there's a greater chance that the car will stay on the groove for the whole run. If the car gets off the groove while moving too fast, it will spin out of control.

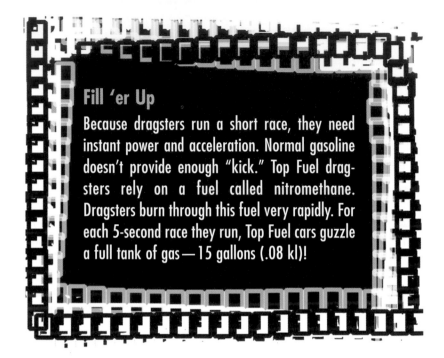

Fill 'er Up

Because dragsters run a short race, they need instant power and acceleration. Normal gasoline doesn't provide enough "kick." Top Fuel dragsters rely on a fuel called nitromethane. Dragsters burn through this fuel very rapidly. For each 5-second race they run, Top Fuel cars guzzle a full tank of gas—15 gallons (.08 kl)!

Hot-rod tires look completely different depending on whether they are used in the front or in the back. The two in front are thin. They look like bicycle wheels. Their purpose is to steer. The two rear tires, called slicks, are completely bald. It looks as if their treads have worn off. Their purpose is to generate speed and traction.

The rear wheels of a Top Fuel dragster are designed to generate high speeds while maintaining traction with the road surface.

The sidewalls, or sides, of most racecar tires tend to be hard. That's because they need to withstand a lot of pressure when they turn tight corners. But dragsters run an almost perfectly straight race, so they can have softer tires. The soft sidewalls of Top Fuel cars allow more of a tire's rubber to grip the track's surface at all times. This increases traction. More traction means higher speeds.

MEASURES OF SAFETY

Driving Top Fuel dragsters can be dangerous. It's not unusual for hot rods to smoke or catch fire. NHRA officials work hard to make the cars as safe as possible. A metal safety cage surrounds each cockpit. The cage protects drivers from getting crushed in a crash. Inside each hot rod is a fire extinguisher system. If a fire breaks out, within seconds the system automatically hoses down the engine and cockpit. But racers don't have to sit still and

Top Fuel dragsters use a metal safety cage that covers the cockpit to protect the driver in case of a crash.

wait to be rescued. Top Fuel dragsters have escape hatches in their roofs in case drivers need to make a quick getaway. Both Top Fuel dragsters and Funny Cars have parachutes in the rear. When the race ends, the driver pushes a button to release the parachute. As the parachute swells with air, the dragster brakes. The quicker the dragster brakes, the less chance the car has of skidding off the strip and crashing.

Record Times

When it comes to speed records, fans can count on hot-rodders to deliver the goods. Here is a time line of some smashing speeds, who set them, and when.

SPEED	WHO	WHEN
150 mph (241 km/h)	Lloyd Scott	1955
200 mph (322 km/h)	Don "Big Daddy" Garlits	1967
250 mph (402 km/h)	Don "Big Daddy" Garlits	1975
300 mph (483 km/h)	Kenny Bernstein	1992
330 mph (531 km/h)	Tony Schumacher	1999

Funny Cars, like this one, are similar to Top Fuel dragsters in that they both do not have brakes. Instead, they use parachutes that the drivers release just after they cross the finish line.

Let the Race BEGIN

Do you think you know all there is to know about drag racing? Do you think it's just fast cars zooming down a strip, and whoever hits the highest speed wins? Actually, drag racing is a complex sport.

E.T. PHONE HOME?

Before a race, each hot rod makes a few trial runs. The elapsed time of each run is noted. Elapsed time, or E.T., is a measure of how long it takes for a hot rod to get to the finish line. The driver's mechanics compare all of the trial E.T.s. Then they guess what the car's E.T. will be during the competition. That guess is called a dial-in.

In some drag racing categories, when two

This drag racer is making one of several trial runs so that she will be able to figure out her elapsed time.

cars compete, race officials compare the dial-ins. From this, they determine which car gets a head start. For instance, if Car A records a dial-in of 17, and Car B has a dial-in of 15, then Car A will get a 2-second head start. If Cars A and B finish in a tie, the victory goes to Car B, because Car A didn't make up its head start.

FASTEST ISN'T ALWAYS FIRST

So why not just guess a really high dial-in? Say you know you can run the race in 15 seconds. Why not just dial in 18 instead, and get a huge head start?

If a dragster runs the race with a quicker E.T. than its dial-in, it loses. This is called a breakout. So if Car A's dial-in is 19 and Car B's is 15, Car A gets a 4-second head start. But if Car A runs the race with an E.T. of 16, it loses—even if it crossed the finish line first. So

A dragster takes part in a time trial.

drivers must make precise guesses on their dial-in times.

This is certainly a complex system. But it is used so that cars that perform at very different levels can compete in a fair contest.

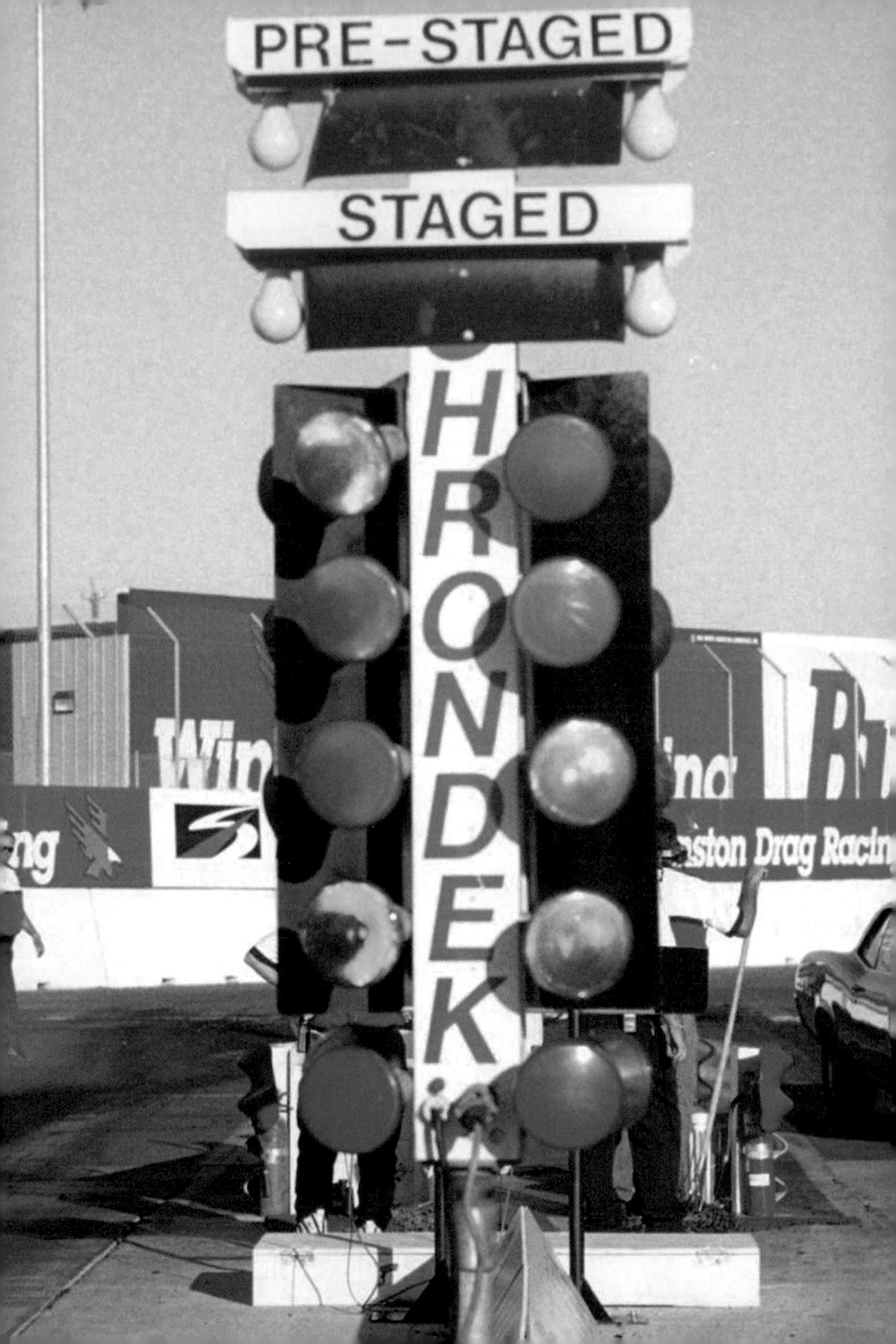
PRE-STAGED
STAGED
HRONDEK

WAITING FOR CHRISTMAS

When hot-rodders set themselves at the starting line, they stare at two columns of paired lights. These lights are nicknamed Christmas Trees. The top three pairs of amber (yellow) lights signal first. This means the race is just about to begin. Less than half a second later, the fourth pair of lights flash on. These lights are green. They signal the start of the race.

Tension builds at every race. Drivers' heartbeats go from 120 beats per minute before the race to 205 beats per minute when the Christmas Tree shines green. Reaction time is critical. Drivers must make their moves at the instant that the amber lights dim and the green lights begin to shine.

There is one last light on the Christmas Tree—a red one. It signals that a driver's front wheels have crossed the starting line before the race has begun. If you see the red light during a drag race, it means that a driver has

The lights used to signal drivers are nicknamed Christmas Trees.

fouled out. It's an automatic disqualification, and the driver's day is done.

After two days of qualifying runs, sixteen cars are chosen as the top competitors. Sunday is their day of sudden elimination. Two cars

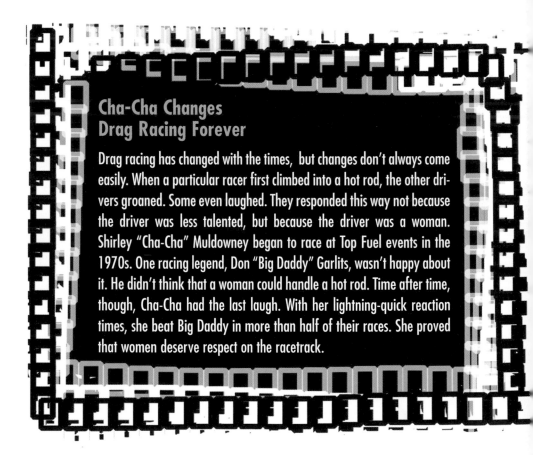

Cha-Cha Changes Drag Racing Forever

Drag racing has changed with the times, but changes don't always come easily. When a particular racer first climbed into a hot rod, the other drivers groaned. Some even laughed. They responded this way not because the driver was less talented, but because the driver was a woman. Shirley "Cha-Cha" Muldowney began to race at Top Fuel events in the 1970s. One racing legend, Don "Big Daddy" Garlits, wasn't happy about it. He didn't think that a woman could handle a hot rod. Time after time, though, Cha-Cha had the last laugh. With her lightning-quick reaction times, she beat Big Daddy in more than half of their races. She proved that women deserve respect on the racetrack.

Shirley "Cha-Cha" Muldowney was the first woman to race Top Fuel dragsters.

race each other. The winner moves on to the next round. The loser goes home. This process is repeated for several rounds. The last car still driving at the end of the day is crowned champion, or top eliminator.

DRIVING STRATEGIES

Although runs begin and end in seconds, the contest is very much one of mental ability. Drivers must keep their concentration. At the same time, they have to be relaxed. For example, it's important to hold the wheel firmly during a run. But if a driver grips it too hard, an oversteer can occur. This happens when the wheel jerks too sharply. It often results in a spinout.

Distractions are a driver's worst enemy. If you let your mind wander, you are bound to lose. Drivers say the best way to concentrate on winning is not to think about winning. Racing legends became champions by focusing on just one thing at the starting line: a quick reaction time.

Drivers need to keep their concentration focused on what they are doing during a race.

A Day at the RACES

Drag racing grows bigger each year. If you're interested, you can catch the excitement on TV. Networks such as ABC, ESPN, and The Nashville Network (TNN) carry every national event. However, nothing measures up to the experience of being there. Newly remodeled strips—like the Gateway International Raceway in St. Louis—are always opening. Or check out a brand-new dragstrip, like the Route 66 Raceway in Joliet, Illinois.

Wherever you go, buy tickets in advance. And come early! Festivities last all weekend. The first days are filled with qualifying runs. This is when it's decided who will compete in the elimination rounds. Of course, Sunday is the main event. That's the day when the top eliminator is decided.

Drivers take part in elimination rounds to see who will make it to the main event.

The sport of drag racing is very fan-friendly. Event organizers know that not every spectator is an expert. So after big runs, an announcer will explain why a driver won or lost. When the day is over, you can walk by the pits. There's a good chance that a hot-rodder will answer a question or sign your program. Maybe you'll even get the champion's autograph.

GET ON TRACK!

If what you see at the raceways inspires you, there may be a place for you in a hot-rod cockpit. A great place to get started is the Junior Drag Racing League (JDRL). This organization, founded in 1992, is part of the NHRA. It is geared toward giving young people a chance to race. Over the years, kids from every state have joined the league to try hot-rod racing. Today, more than four thousand young people compete in the JDRL each year.

In the JDRL, young people ages eight to

NHRA Junior Dragsters and the kids who drive them must meet strict safety requirements. Cars have to have roll cages. The drivers must wear helmets and other safety equipment, and the cars must pass a technical inspection at every race.

For kids from ages eight to seventeen, a Junior Dragster is the ultimate toy.

seventeen may compete as drivers The rules of the junior circuit are quite similar to those of the professional circuit. Of course, not everything is the same. The drag strip is one eighth of a mile (.4 km), instead of one quarter (.2 km). Junior dragsters can attain speeds of 85 mph (137 km/h). Top drivers run the strip in less than 8 seconds. As in the pro categories, JDRL racing is open to everyone. It is divided into age groups, and boys and girls race one another. In fact, one out of every four JDRL drivers is a girl. JDRL is a great program to be a part of. Members have a lot of fun. But there is some serious competition, too. The racing year concludes with two Conference Finals. One is held on each coast of the United States. Winners receive thousands of dollars in scholarship money.

Make sure to check out the Resources section of this book when you finish reading. There is information on the JDRL. It tells you how to become a part of hod-rod action. Maybe someday you can race into the record books.

NEW WORDS

accelerate to pick up speed

aerodynamics a measure of how air affects an object's movement

airfoil a fixed wing that is mounted on the rear of all Top Fuel cars

chassis the supporting frame of a car

classification a system of grouping hot rods

downforce a type of energy that pushes objects toward the ground

elapsed time (E.T.) the measure of how long it takes for a hot rod to get to the finish line

grip to hold firmly

groove an area of sticky rubber that covers the center of drag strips

hot-rodders the nickname given to the very first drag racers

innovator a person who does something in a new way

roll bar a safety feature that prevents drivers from getting crushed if their car flips

slicks the rear tires of a dragster

straightaways the long strips of track that do not have curves

For Further READING

Cockerham, Paul W. *Drag Racing.* Broomall, PA: Chelsea House Publishers, 1997.

McKenn, A.T. *Drag Racing.* Minneapolis, MN: ABDO Publishing Company, 1998.

Sakkis, Tony. *Drag Racing Legends.* Osceola, WI: MBI Publishing Company, 1996.

RESOURCES

International Hot Rod Association

www.ihra.com

This is the official site of the International Hot Rod Association. Check out this site to learn more about this organization, including information about its staff, sponsors, drivers, and member tracks. The site also provides schedules of National, Divisional, and Junior Dragster events.

National Hot Rod Association

www.nhra.com

This is the official site of the National Hot Rod Association. It includes information about drivers, events, and current racing news. If you're interested in racing, it also provides details about the Junior Drag Racing League.

INDEX

INDEX

ABOUT THE AUTHOR

Matthew Pitt is a freelance writer who has written books and short stories for teenagers and adults.